Glastonbury Comes Home

Glastonbury Tails Series

Tim Vincent & Gordon Fanthom

First Printing, 2019

ISBN: 9781697556407

Printed in the United States of America

Dedication

For
Joseph Edward Fanthom ' a true Gentleman '

Glastonbury Comes Home

Table of Contents

Glastonbury was a very lucky cat. He lived in a beautiful palace.

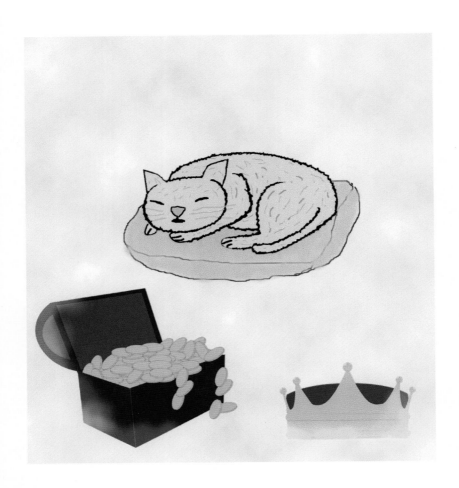

He had everything he needed or wanted. He even slept on a golden pillow.

He was a wealthy cat. But a
sad cat. A lonely cat.

One night the sky got very
dark. There was a lot of
thunder and lightning.

Glastonbury got very scared and hid under his golden pillow.

Suddenly there was a loud
bang and a bright flash of
light.

Water rushed into the palace.
Glastonbury clung to his
golden pillow.

The water rose higher and higher and Glastonbury was swept away.

Glastonbury was very scared, but he soon fell asleep. He dreamed of his beautiful palace.

The next morning, when
Glastonbury awoke, the sun
was shining and the birds
were tweeting.

The Pillow drifted on
through forests and under
bridges. 'How peaceful',
thought Glastonbury.

Suddenly the water roared
and started to foam angrily.
Glastonbury was scared. He
was speeding towards some
huge rocks.

20

Glastonbury fell off his pillow and into the water. He closed his eyes and screamed very loudly.

Then, as if by magic,
Glastonbury started moving
up and out of the water.

Glastonbury was saved! He lay in a puddle of water on the bank of the river. He was a very lucky cat.

'Hello,' said a kindly voice.
'I'm Grease Monkey, come
to my place and get dry.'

Grease Monkey's home was
a strange place. There were
lots of machines lying
around.

In the middle of the
machines, sat a dark
handsome cat. 'Hello,' he
said, 'I'm Bone.'

'This is my home. I live here with Grease Monkey.' Said Bone. 'please stay with us and be my friend.' He pleaded.

Glastonbury saw their
smiling faces and knew this
was a place he could be
happy and grow old in.
Glastonbury was home!

Glastonbury and Bone
became best of friends and
had many adventures
together.

Like all cats, Glastonbury
and Bone loved singing at
night. But, Grease Monkey
didn't like it much so he
threw his boot at them.

Bone soon got busy writing the Glastonbury song, which is all about his best friend.

You can sing-along to the Glastonbury song. The words are on the next few pages….

Glastonbury the cat faced cat
The cat faced cat, the cat faced cat
Glastonbury the cat faced cat
The cat faced cat, the cat faced cat

He's got a face just like an old cat
He's got a face just like an old cat
He's got a face just like an old cat
He's got a face just like an old cat

Glastonbury the cat faced cat
The cat faced cat, the cat faced cat
Glastonbury the cat faced cat
The cat faced cat, the cat faced cat

He's got a face just like an old cat
That's because he's just an old cat
He's got a face just like an old cat
That's because he's just an old cat

Glastonbury the cat faced cat
The cat faced cat, the cat faced cat
Glastonbury the cat faced cat
The cat faced cat, the cat faced cat

He's got a face just like an old cat
He knows just when to skit and scat
He's got a face just like an old cat
He knows just when to skit and scat

Glastonbury the cat faced cat
The cat faced cat, the cat faced cat
Glastonbury the cat faced cat
The cat faced cat, the cat faced cat

It's not all about this and that
It's just a story of an old cat
It's not all about this and that
It's just a story of an old cat

Keep singing along with Glastonbury and Bone and watch out for their further adventures!

The End

Download the Glastonbury
song from:

http://timvincentauthor.co.uk/glastonbury-tails/

Printed in Poland
by Amazon Fulfillment
Poland Sp. z o.o., Wrocław

49380886R00023